A CASE OF BLIND FEAR

Malibu Graphics, Inc.

Other Books Available From Malibu Graphics

Dinosaurs For Hire: Guns 'N Lizards
At last, a sensitive tale of teen-age angst and the trauma of growing up in middle class America. Just kidding! It's really about Dinosaurs with automatic weapons. By Tom Mason. Illustrated by Bryon Carson and Mike Roberts.

The Three Stooges: The Knuckleheads Return
Nyuk! Nyuk! Nyuk! Those knuckleheads are back in a collection of seven slapstick adventures!
Edited by Tom Mason.

Abbot And Costello: The Classic Comics
Bud Abbot and Lou Costello are reunited in this collection of 20 classic comic stories from their heyday.
Edited by Tom Mason.

Spicy Detective Stories
A classic collection of seven two-fisted 1930s pulp detective stories from the pages of Spicy Detective magazine.
Edited By Tom Mason.

Frankenstein Graphic Novel
Based on Mary Shelley's classic novel of horror, Frankenstein: The Modern Prometheus includes originally published material from Eternity's critically acclaimed Frankenstien mini-series. Adapted by Martin Powell, art by Patrick Olliffe.

The Trouble With Girls
Lester Girls would like nothing more than to curl up with a good book in a quiet, suburban bungalow. Instead, he's stuck with a ceaseless round of luscious babes, high adventure, uncountable riches, and break-neck action.
By Will Jacobs and Gerard Jones. Illustrated by Tim Hamilton and Dave Garcia.

The Trouble With Girls Volume Two: My Name Is Girls
Adventurer, hero, tycoon, lover...Lester Girls is all of this and more. Yet, he is not a happy man. All he wants are the simple things in life--a mousy wife, a routine job, and a pair of sensible shoes. For Lester Girls, the simplest things are the hardest to attain! By Will Jacobs and Gerard Jones. Illustrated by Tim Hamilton.

Scimidar Book One: Pleasure And Pain
She's a poet, a lover, a dreamer. She's also a sexy, empathic tracker in the year 2005. Absorbing the emotions of those around her, she is a walking time bomb. She is Scimidar. By R.A. Jones. Illustrated by Rob Davis with Albert Val and James Baldwin. Mature subject matter. Not intended for children.

Scarlet In Gaslight
Sherlock Holmes meets Dracula in the strangest case of his career! By Martin Powell and Seppo Makinen.

Dark Wolf
Priest by day, vengeful killer by night. By R.A. Jones and Butch Burcham.

Plan Nine From Outer Space
John Wooley adapts the "Worst Movie Ever Made." Illustrated by Stan Timmons and Bruce McCorkindale.

Sherlock Holmes-A Case of Blind Fear
Graphic Album
Published by Malibu Graphics, Inc.
1355 Lawrence Dr. #212
Newbury Park, CA 91320.
805/499-3015.
Printed in the USA. First Printing.
ISBN# 0-944735-50-9 $9.95 • $11.95 In Canada

> For Ron Fortier
> Fellow Sherlockian
> Acclaimed Author
> Forever A Friend

Sherlock Holmes-A Case Of Blind Fear © copyright 1990 Martin Powell. Introduction copyright ©1990 Martin Powell. Artwork © copyright 199 Seppo Makinen. Any similarity to persons living or dead is purely coincidental. With the exception of artwork used for review purposes, none of the contents of this publication may be reprinted without the consent of Malibu Graphics, Inc. All other contents ©1990 Malibu Graphics, Inc.

Based on the Sherlock Holmes characters created by Sir Arthur Conan Doyle. The Sherlock Holmes characters appear by arrangement with Dame Jean Conan Doyle.

Sherlock Holmes A Case Of Blind Fear

Martin Powell
Writer

Seppo Makinen
Artist

Pat Brosseau
Letterer

Dan & David Day
Cover

Dave Olbrich
Publisher

Chris Ulm
Editor-In-Chief

Mickie Villa
Associate Editor

Dan Danko
Editorial Assistant

Tom Mason
Creative Director

Figuring Out The Fascination

A Foreword By Martin Powell

I've long been fascinated by Sherlock Holmes.

It started when I was in the sixth grade and an English teacher assigned a reading of the A. Conan Doyle story "The Norwood Builder" to my class. Even before my eyes met the first work I tingled with excitement as Miss Berne described the tale; a 19th century mystery, and its main character, the detective Sherlock Holmes. I listened in boyish seriousness while learning about this remarkable man who had become world famous because of the power of his intellect.

I sat slightly astounded. Imagine! Being able to tell intimate even secretive things about total strangers with just the slightest glance at them! When I finally got down to actually reading the story I was even more charmed, particularly impressed with Holmes' devilishly clever, yet ridiculously simple solution of the mystery.

Enriched as I suddenly was, however, this new love affair was not to blossom. Not yet. I was too busy doing the things a boy growing up in the sixties was meant to do: reading tons of comics, watching *Lost In Space* and *Twilight Zone*, listening to the Beatles, writing letters to my brother in Vietnam, marvelling at men walking on the moon, playing Dracula with my cousins in a country family grave yard, and literally losing myself in a smallish, dimly lighted, over-crammed local library, where I nearly exhausted my imagination with thick books of dinosaurs, ghosts, Frankenstein monsters and blood sucking bats.

I passed over A. Conan Doyle in those days for H. G. Wells, and discovered the original parent of Claude Rains' cinematic creation in *The Invisible Man*.

Little did I realize he and the detective Holmes would one day be meeting each other.

In this limited-series I've attempted not so much to exploit each author's creation as much as reflect their own magic, and build on their already legendary foundations.

The reader will find Sherlock Holmes himself more masterful, more in control here then he was in my previous venture, *Scarlet In Gaslight*; and Dr. Watson plays a much more demanding role in this adventure (in opposition to Holmes, in fact). Of course, the madman Griffin lurks, usually unseen, in these pages. Conan Doyle and Wells never dreamt of the bizarre bond that linked the two medical men together. Now the "truth" is told.

Conan Doyle purists will be pleased, I hope, with my portrayals of Colonel Sebastian Moran, the late Professor Moriarty's perverse successor, and rare cameos of the brilliantly explosive George Edward Challenger and the magnificently eccentric Mycroft Holmes. Sir Arthur created so many wonderful characters the difficulty here was in choosing, not searching.

I'm certain many a Holmes fan will raise a speculative eyebrow at the return of Irene Adler, *the woman*, into Holmes' life. I know many will be protectively skeptical when considering the Great Detective as the focus of a possible love affair; whether I handle their relationship realistically is up to the opinion of the reader.

This is a tale of madness, murder, forbidden love and eternal friendship. In all, artist Seppo Makinen and I very much enjoyed this story. Although it didn't flow creatively as easily as did *Scarlet In Gaslight*, we believe it is somewhat richer in characterization and atmosphere; two absolutely essential elements to any Sherlock Holmes story.

We hope you will agree.

Martin Powell
January, 1990

"THAT'S THE ONE, MR. HOLMES--HE WAS AT VICTORIA STATION."

"SURELY SCOTLAND YARD MUST HAVE FORMED SOME OPINION OF ALL THIS?"

"HMM. AS LESTRADE HIMSELF WOULD SAY--THAT DOES FIT THE FACTS."

"SO I BELIEVED, SIR, UNTIL THIS CHEMIST SHOPPE AFFAIR. THE BURGLARY WAS GENUINE."

"WELL, INSPECTOR LESTRADE BELIEVES WE ARE IN THE MIDST OF A WEIRD EPIDEMIC...SOME MYSTERIOUS PLAGUE, INDUCING HYSTERICAL HALLUCINATIONS."

"INDEED. A CRIME IS FINALLY COMMITTED--I DON'T COUNT THE GHOSTLY VOYEUR OR THE FLYING FRUIT. HAVE YOU THE LIST OF CHEMICALS TAKEN?"

"WE CONSULTED DR. WATSON AFTER THE THEFT--HE IDENTIFIED THE DRUGS AS VERY RARE AND OBSCURE. HE ADMITTED PUZZLEMENT AT THE RANDOM SELECTION, ESPECIALLY WHEN OPIUM AND COCAINE WERE EASILY WITHIN EQUAL REACH."

"AH, I NEVER SEEM TO GET WATSON'S LIMITS! I FEAR I'VE SEEN LITTLE OF HIM SINCE COLONEL MORAN'S INSANITY HEARING LAST YEAR, AND ONCE AGAIN I AM IN HIS DEBT."

"THANK YOU FOR YOUR TIME, MR. HOLMES. I WILL KEEP YOU ABREAST OF ANY NEW DEVELOPMENTS."

"PLEASE DO, INSPECTOR. CRIME HAS BECOME SINGULARLY UNINTERESTING SINCE THE DEATH OF PROFESSOR MORIARTY..."

"...THE DAYS OF THE GREAT CASES ARE PAST, BUT I FIND THIS BUSINESS NOT WITHOUT MERIT--AND I SHALL BE VERY SURPRISED IF I HAVEN'T HEARD FROM YOU WITHIN A WEEK."

"THE DOOR HAD TO BE FORCED. THE ROOM WAS *EMPTY*. AND SO MR. JAMES PHILLIMORE, WHO, STEPPING INTO HIS ROOM TO GET HIS UMBRELLA, WAS *NEVER* SEEN AGAIN IN THIS WORLD."

"THE MEN MADE A COMPLETE SEARCH OF THE ROOM?"

"YES, MR. HOLMES. THE WINDOWS WERE FASTENED FROM THE *INNER SIDE*. THE KEY STILL REMAINED IN THE DOOR."

ALL THAT WAS LEFT OF MR. PHILLIMORE WAS THIS PILE OF CLOTHING!

SO I OBSERVE. MINNIE, ARE YOU CERTAIN THESE ARE THE *ACTUAL GARMENTS* PHILLIMORE WAS WEARING BEFORE HE VANISHED?

HE ONLY HAD THE ONE SET THAT I KNOW OF, SIR.

HMM. INSPECTOR, WERE YOU AWARE THAT MANY OF THESE CHEMICALS MATCH THE *RARE POTIONS* STOLEN IN THE HARRISON BURGLARY?

WHAT--! ARE YOU SURE?

"REASONABLY SO. MINNIE, TELL ME OF MR. HALL'S SUDDEN DEATH."

"WELL, SIR, HE SEEMED RIGHT SHAKEN ABOUT THE WHOLE THING-- SEEMED TO BE LOSING HIS NERVE, EVEN AS HE FIRST WENT INTO THE ROOM."

"WAS HE USUALLY A NERVOUS MAN?"

"NOT AT ALL, BUT THE GLOOM OF THE PLACE DID RATHER POKE AT YOU, SIR. THEN, THERE WAS THAT WAY HE TURNED HIS HEAD, STARING LIKE SOMETHING JUST *SPOKE* TO HIM."

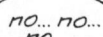

"...PARTICULARLY OPTICAL DENSITY.

"FOR FOURTEEN YEARS I WORKED BLINDLY, UNTIL I HAD CREATED A CHEMICAL METHOD WHEREBY BLOOD COULD BE MADE COLORLESS.

"ALMOST IMMEDIATELY I TOOK THE DRUGS.

"I HADN'T EXPECTED THE PAIN. MY VERY VEINS FELT ON FIRE.

"I STRUGGLED DIZZILY THROUGH FITS OF FAINTING AND WAKING...

"...FINALLY MANAGING THE EFFORT TO GAZE INTO MY SHAVING-GLASS.

"IT WAS THE LAST TIME I WOULD EVER SEE MYSELF.

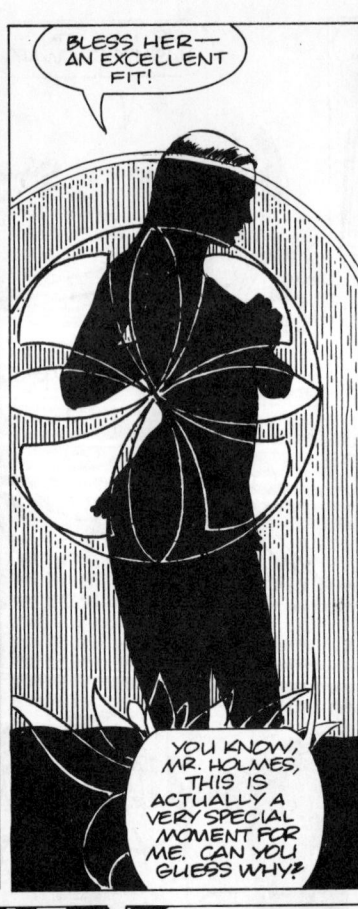

"HIS GREAT DEVOTION AND COURAGE SUCCEEDED IN BRINGING ME SAFELY ACROSS THE BRITISH LINES — AT TREMENDOUS PERSONAL RISK."

"I OWE HIM MY LIFE."

"I OWE HIM EVERYTHING I'VE BECOME."

"THAT SAME HEROIC ORDERLY WAS..."

"...MURRAY GRIFFIN."

MY OBLIGATION TO HIM HAS AFFECTED MY JUDGEMENT...AND HAS ENDANGERED *YOU*. GRIFFIN IS MORE UNSTABLE THAN I DARED TO ADMIT — EVEN TO MYSELF.

I'VE BEEN A *FOOL*.

NO, DEAREST...

YOU'RE A VERY GOOD MAN.

DID YOU HEAR SOMETHING?

STARTLING WOMAN.
REMARKABLE WOMAN.

SELFISHNESS OR NOT...
...SHE HAS JUST SAVED OUR LIVES.

THESE MEN BELONG TO COLONEL MORAN? THE SUCCESSOR TO MORIARTY? I THOUGHT--
THAT HE WAS IMPRISONED, HOPELESSLY INSANE. INDEED, THE ENGLISH COURTS BELIEVE SO, TOO.
ALL RIGHT, JENNINGS--THE GAME IS UP!

THE THRILL IS INDESCRIBABLE.
I STALK TOWARD THEM, MY NAKED FEET PADDING SILENTLY ON THE COBBLESTONE, NOT FEELING THE ICY RAIN. THEY DON'T HEAR ME.

THEY CAN'T SEE ME.

I WANT TO LAUGH.

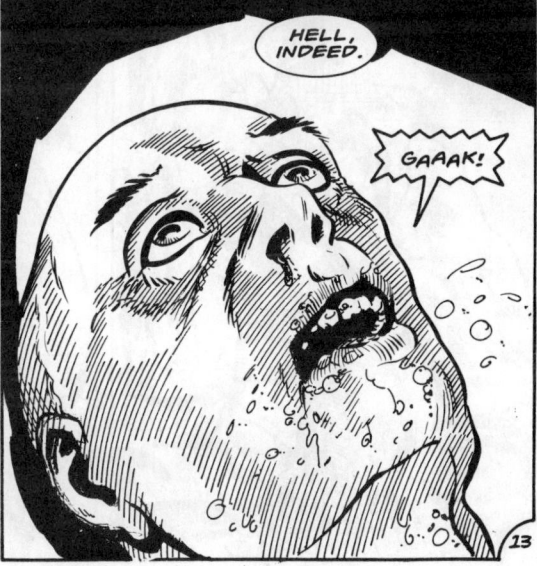

Acknowledgements

It wouldn't be right to let this book go to press without properly thanking those responsible for its shaping and production: I owe a great debt to Dame Jean Conan Doyle, who has very generously allowed me a splendid creative freedom in dealing with her father's characters; thanks to editor Chris Ulm and Eternity Comics, who kindly asked for more; my gratitude to Ray Bradbury, always an inspiration, special appreciation to friend and Holmes scholar, Wayne R. Smith; my thanks and friendship to Patrick Olliffe, Ron Fortier, Kathy West, Bobbie Stamper, Sally Shatto, Shannon Conder, Alan Madison, Myron Harrod, Ronda Castle, Alan Sissom, Dan Tyree, Jim Robertson, Carla Lovo, Sandy Erbele, James McGill, Lonnie Hampton, Greg Wathen, Robert Greer, and Don and Maggie Thompson for their warm enthusiasm and generous interest regarding this project; I'm indebted to Seppo Makinen and Mike Friedrich, both determined to help me grow; and to the gentle patience of Martha, my wife, an ideal writer's mate.

Martin Powell

• GRAPHIC NOVELS •

ABBOTT & COSTELLO
The crazy comedy duo is back in this classic collection of the misadventures from the '40s and '50s.

CHINA SEA
An epic adventure in the tradition of Terry and the Pirates.

DINOSAURS FOR HIRE
Three gun-crazy Dinosaurs on the loose as private eyes!

FU MANCHU
Sax Rohmer's villainous creation stars in two classic adventures.

NINJA HIGH SCHOOL
One boy, two girls, giant robots. Trouble ahead.

PERRY MASON
The world's most famous lawyer stars in four classic cases.

PLAN 9 FROM OUTER SPACE
The only authorized adaptation of the worst movie ever made!

SCARLET IN GASLIGHT
An all new epic adventure pitting the world's greatest detective against Cound Dracula!

SCIMIDAR
The adventures of a female bounty hunter in the year 2005. Contains nudity and sexual situations.

SHERLOCK HOLMES
The world's greatest detective is featured in 6 full length adventures from the newspaper strip of the '50s.

SPICY DETECTIVE STORIES
Illustrated fiction from the naughty pulps of the '30s and '40s.

SPICY TALES
Uncensored comics from the pulps of the '30s.

TEEN ANGST
A treasury of pre-code '50s romance stories.

THREE STOOGES
Nyuk! Nyuk! Nyuk! The Knuckleheads return in collection of their looney antics.

THREE MUSKETEERS
All for one and one for all in this new adaptation of the classic Dumas novel.

TIGER-X
In the late 20th Century, a Soviet invasion has split the U.S. in two.

TROUBLE WITH GIRLS
Lester Girls longs for the quiet life, if only the fabulous babes, ninja assassins, and relentless reporter Maxi Scoops could leave him alone.

WAR OF THE WORLDS
The Aliens Have Landed! Based on the H.G. Wells novel.

Don't cut up your comics! A photocopy of this coupon is acceptable!

ABBOTT & COSTELLO___$17.00 * CHINA SEA___$7.00
NINJA HIGH SCHOOL___$9.00 * TIGER-X___$10.00
DINOSAURS FOR HIRE Guns N' Lizards___$7.00 * Dinosaurs Rule!___$7.00
FU MANCHU___$14.00 * PERRY MASON___$18.00 • PLAN 9___$6.00
SCARLET IN GASLIGHT___$8.00 • SCIMIDAR___$11.00
SHERLOCK HOLMES___$20.00 • SPICY TALES___$11.00
SPICY DETECTIVE STORIES___$8.00 • TEEN ANGST___$15.00
THREE STOOGES___$17.00 * THREE MUSKETEERS___$11.00
TROUBLE WITH GIRLS (Vol. One)___$9.00 • MY NAME IS GIRLS (Vol. Two)___$9.00
WAR OF THE WORLDS___$11.00

I certify that I am over 18 (required for Scimidar)

Signature_____
Name (please print)_____
Address_____
City_____ State_____ Zip_____

Minimum order: $10.00 All prices include postage (US orders only--Canada and Mexico add $1.00 per order. Overseas add $3.00 per order). Please allow 4-6 weeks for delivery. Do not send cash. Make money orders and checks payable to Malibu Graphics, Inc., 1355 Lawrence Drive #212, Newbury Park, CA 91320. Please list alternates.

ALSO AVAILABLE FROM MALIBU GRAPHICS

Minimum Order: $10.00. Prices include postage (US orders only—Canada and Mexico add $1.00 per order, Overseas add $3.00 per order). Comics are shipped in plastic bags. **List alternates.** Money Orders and Checks only. Please do not send cash. Send orders and make checks payable to: MALIBU GRAPHICS, 1355 Lawrence Drive #212, Newbury Park, CA 91320

ADVENTURERS
Book II #7 $3.00
Book III #1-4
$3.00 ea

APACHE DICK
#1-2 $2.50ea

ARGONAUTS
#2-4 $1.00ea

BAD AXE
#1-3 $3.00ea

BATTLE ARMOR
#3 $1.00

BIG PRIZE
#1-2 $1.00ea

BLADE OF SHURIKEN
#2-3,5 $1.00ea

BLIND FEAR
Sherlock Holmes returns! All new!
#1-4 $2.50ea

BLOODBROTHERS
#1-4 $1.00ea

BLOODWING
#1-5 $1.00ea

BODY COUNT
Move over Freddy!
#1-3 $3.00 each

BUSHIDO
#1-4 $2.50ea

CAPTAIN HARLOCK
#1 $3.00 #2-5 $2.50ea
Full color poster
$6.95

CHARLIE CHAN
#1-3, 5, 6 $2.50ea

COSMIC HEROES
Buck Rogers
#1-4, 6, 8-11
$2.50ea

CRIME CLASSICS
The Shadow returns
#3-13 $2.50ea

DARK WOLF
(Mini-Series)
#1 $6.00 #2-4
$3.00ea
(Regular Series)
#1 $3.00 #2-4, 6-14 $2.50ea
Annual #1 $3.00

DEMON HUNTER
#1-4 $1.00ea

DINOSAURS FOR HIRE
#1 (2nd print), #2-4, 6-9 $2.50ea
Fall Classic #1
$3.00
Guns N'Lizards
Graphic Novel
$7.00

DRACULA
All New!
#1-3 $3.00ea

DRAGONFORCE
#5-13 $2.50ea
Chronicles #1-5
$3.50ea

EDGAR ALLAN POE
Pit/ Pendulum $2.50
Mask/Red Death
$2.50
Rue Morgue $2.50
Black Cat $2.50

ELFLORD
#23-31 $2.50ea

EX-MUTANTS
(Original Series)
#1(Signed by Ron Lim) $10.00 ea
#6-7 $2.50ea

EX-MUTANTS: The Shattered Earth Chronicles
#1 $3.00
#2-10,12-14
$2.50ea
Annual #1 $3.00
Pin-Up Book #1
$3.00

FIFTIES TERROR
Pre-Code Horror
#1, 3-4, 6 $2.50ea

FIST OF GOD
#2-4 $2.50ea

FRANKENSTEIN
#1-3 $2.50ea

FRIGHT
#1,3, 4-12 $2.50ea

GUN FURY
#1-10 $2.50ea
#1 (Signed) $5.00

HAMSTER VICE
#1-2 $1.00ea

HEADLESS HORSEMAN
#1-2 $2.50ea

HELLBENDER
#1 $2.50

HOWL
#1-2 $2.50ea

HUMAN GARGOYLES
#1-4 $2.50ea

JACK THE RIPPER
All new!
#1-3 $2.50ea

JAKE THRASH
The Complete Saga
(80 pages)
$4.50

KIKU SAN
#1-6 $2.50ea

LEATHER & LACE
#2-8 (Over 18 Only—state age when ordering)
$3.00ea
#2-8 (General)
$2.50ea

MEN IN BLACK
#1-3 $2.50 ea

MONSTER FRAT HOUSE
#1 $2.50

NEW HUMANS
Shattered Earth
#2-15 $2.50ea
Annual #1 $3.50

NINJA
#1,2,6, 7,10-12
$1.00ea
Special #1 $1.00

NINJA HIGH SCHOOL
Ben Dunn
#6-11,13-15
$2.50ea
#1 (60 pp) $3.50
#2-3, 3 1/2, 4
$2.50ea
Graphic Novel
$9.00
Graphic Novel
(signed) $15.00

OUTLANDER
#1 $1.00

PRIVATE EYES
The Saint returns.
#1-3 $2.50ea
#4 (60 pp) $3.50
#5 (60 pp) $3.50
#6 (60pp) $3.50

PUBLIC ENEMIES
Classic Crime
#1-2 $4.00 ea

RETIEF
Keith Laumer's famous creation stars in all new adventures!
#1-2 $2.50ea

RIPPER
#1-5 $3.00ea

ROBIN HOOD
#1-2 $2.50ea

ROBOTECH II: THE SENTINELS
#1 (2nd printing) #2-6,8-12 $2.50ea
Wedding Special
#1-2 $2.50ea
Full color poster
$6.95

ROBOTECH II: THE SENTINELS The Malcontent Uprisings
#1-4 $2.50ea
Full color poster
$6.95

SCIMIDAR
#1-2 $2.50ea
Book II #1 $6.00
(first printing) Book II #1 (2nd printing)
$2.75
Book II #3 $3.00
Book III #1-2
$3.00ea

SHATTERED EARTH
#2,4,5,7-9 $2.50ea

SHERLOCK HOLMES
The classic strip from the '50s collected for the first time.
#1-20 $3.00ea
Casebooks #1-2
$2.50ea

SHERLOCK HOLMES
Trade Paperback
6 complete cases
$20.00

SHERLOCK HOLMES of the '30s
#1-3 $3.50ea

SHURIKEN: COLD STEEL
#1-2 $1.50ea
#3-6 $2.50ea

SHURIKEN TEAM-UP
#1 $1.00

SINBAD
New adventures from R.A. Jones and M.C. Wyman.
#1-2 $2.50ea

SOLO EX-MUTANTS
#2,4,5-6 $2.50ea

SPICY DETECTIVE STORIES
The spiciest detective fiction of the '30s, complete with original illustrations.
$8.00

SPICY TALES
Bondage, Murder, and Seduction from the '30s.
#1,8,10-16 $3.00ea

STREET HEROES
#1 $2.50

TEAM: NIPPON
#1-3,5-7 $2.50ea

THREE MUSKETEERS
#1-3 $2.50ea

TIGER-X
Original series
#1, 3 $2.50ea
Book II #1-2
$2.50ea

TOM CORBETT SPACE CADET
#1-2 $2.50ea

TORRID AFFAIRS
'50s romance.
#1-2 $2.50ea
#3-5 (60 pp)
$3.50ea

TROUBLE WITH GIRLS
#9, 11-14 $2.50ea
V2 #5-12 $2.50ea

TWILIGHT AVENGER
#1,3, 5-8 $2.50ea

VAMPYRES
#1-4 $2.50ea

VERDICT
#1-4 $1.00ea

VICTIMS
#1-5 $2.50ea

VIDEO CLASSICS
Here he comes to save the day—
Mighty Mouse!
#1-2 (60pp)
$3.50ea

WALKING DEAD
All new Zombie Horror by Jim Somerville
#1-4 $2.50ea

WARLOCK 5
#16-22 $2.50ea
Book II #1-7
$2.50ea

WARLOCKS
#1 (Special Edition-40 pages) $3.00
#2-10 $2.50ea

WAR OF THE WORLDS
#1-3, 5 $2.50ea

WEREWOLF AT LARGE
#1,3 $2.50ea

WILD KNIGHTS
#1 $3.00
#2-10 $2.50ea

Note: Minimum Order-- $10.00